BEE MINE
I LOVE U
I'm not tea-sing YOU!
YOU'RE MY TYPE
You Light Me Up
I'm a Sucker for You

THE HOUSE OF LOVE

By Adriana Trigiani ♥ Illustrated by Amy June Bates

VIKING

VIKING
An imprint of Penguin Random House LLC, New York

First published in the United States of America by Viking,
an imprint of Penguin Random House LLC, 2021

Visit us online at penguinrandomhouse.com.

Library of Congress Cataloging-in-Publication Data is available.

Manufactured in China

ISBN 9780593203316

10 9 8 7 6 5 4 3 2 1

RRD

Design by Lucia Baez • Text set in Andes Light
The art in this book was created with watercolor, gouache, and pencil on paper.

For my mom and first librarian,
Ida Bonicelli Trigiani.
—A. T.

For houses that have souls.
—A. J. B.

There was an old house at the top of a hill, with many drafty rooms. Inside, there were doors that slammed and stairs that creaked and windows with holes in the glass where the wind whistled through and sounded like music. A tall oak tree grew in the front yard and a sprawling holly tree in the back had plenty of branches for sitting.

A big family lived inside. There were five girls, two boys, a mama, a papa, and a rescue dog named Phyllis. When everyone was home, the rooms exploded with conversation, laughter, and sometimes even an argument.

Mia Valentina was the youngest. February 14th was her favorite day of the year because it was Valentine's Day, and her name meant *My Valentine*!

"Do you think the kids will be home in time for the party?" Mia asked her mother.

"Absolutely," Mama assured her.

"What if Grace's game goes into overtime? What if there's another blizzard and they can't get back over the mountain? What if the car breaks down?" Mia may have been the youngest, but even she knew everything they owned was old.

"There's no more snow in the forecast, and the station wagon is in good shape."

Mia was relieved.

"No one in the Amore family will ever miss Valentine's Day! I'll make sure of that. And you can help."

"I can?" Mia was excited.

Mama and Mia climbed the dusty stairs to the attic. Mama found the bin marked *Valentine's Day.* It was stuffed full with red decorations, long tinsel garlands, glitter hearts, cardboard cupids with velvet arrows, and lace doilies. Mia helped Mama carry the box down to the kitchen. They placed the bin on the antique washing machine.

"Before we decorate, we must do our chores." Mama smiled.

"I will help," Mia Valentina promised.

And she did . . .

VALENTINES
DAY

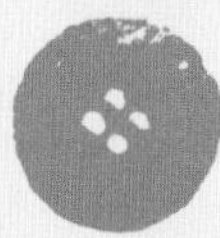

Mia poured bubbly pine soap into a bucket. She dusted the low places where Mama couldn't reach while Mama dusted the high places where Mia couldn't reach. Mia brushed Phyllis until her coat was shiny. And then she tied a shiny red party bow around the pup's neck.

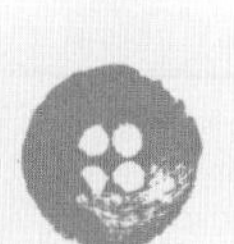
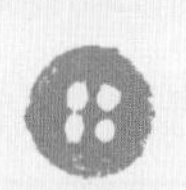

Mia watched as Mama washed the windows, careful to clean around the buttons her daughters had glued over the holes in the glass to keep out the cold.

"Papa wants to get new windows someday, but I like the polka dots myself." Mama stood back and grinned.

"Me too," Mia agreed.

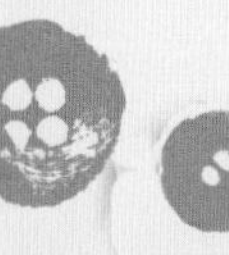

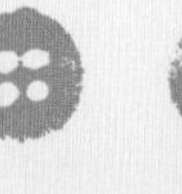

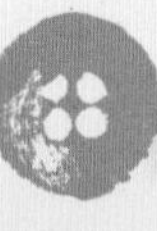
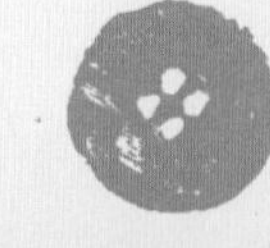

The parlor was the saddest room in the house. Sweeping and polishing and buffing would not help it one bit. "I really have to do something with this room," Mama said. Dull strips of faded brown wallpaper clung to the walls.

"May I finally rip it down?" Mia Valentina asked.

"Yes! But be careful! You never know when you will find a treasure in an old house," Mama said before she went upstairs to straighten up the bedrooms.

Mia stretched and reached and pulled and peeled the brown wallpaper off the parlor walls. When she was done, she rolled a shard of the brown paper into a tube, turned it into a telescope, and spied through the hole like a pirate.

"Ahoy there, Mia!" Mama said from the doorway as she looked around the parlor.

Mia peered at her mother through the paper telescope. Mama looked like she was waving at her through the porthole of a ship.

"I knew you'd find a treasure." Mama beamed.

A pretty wallpaper with hundreds of roses blooming inside a white trellis had been hidden under that dull brown wallpaper all along!

"It's an inside garden!" Mia marveled.

"You made it one! Now this room looks like our Appalachian Mountains in springtime!" Mama said as she went to the foyer and lifted her garden shears out of the basket on the shelf.

Mia watched through a polka-dot window as Mama stood on her tiptoes and snipped a perfect bare limb with many small branches from the oak tree. She waved at Mia with the branch as she trudged across the yard. Mama shoved the bare branch into the cracked pickle crock. "Good one!" she said.

Mama stood on her tiptoes again. This time, she pulled a bag of gumdrops from the shelf. She strung the red, orange, lavender, and green gumdrops with a sewing needle threaded with gold. She made a knot in the thread, which became a loop. Mama handed a gumdrop to Mia, who hung it on the tree. One by one, Mama made them, and Mia hung them. Soon, the candy tree shimmered with sparkling gumdrops.

"Now it's perfect," Mia said.

"I have four extra gumdrops." Mama placed them in Mia's hand. Mia savored the orange gumdrop, gave the green one to Phyllis, and put the other two in her pocket for later.

Happy with their tree, Mia and Mama got to work and festooned the old house with the decorations from the bin. Top to bottom they went, up the stairs, through the rooms, and down the banister.

Every room was bedazzled!

Every corner had a cupid!

Every door, a garland!

Mama opened her purse and pulled out a handful of lollipops. She put them in an empty flower vase, just like real roses. Then Mama tied a red velvet ribbon around the firewood in the kitchen. Mother and daughter unfurled a garland down the hallway on the way to the parlor. "*Hmmm*," Mama said as she stood in the parlor. "This room is missing something."

Mama cut picture frames out of construction paper and hung them on the rose-covered walls. "What do you think, Mia Valentina?"

"The frames are empty."

"What should we do?"

"Let's fill them with valentines," Mia suggested. "One for each of my brothers and sisters."

"They would like that," Mama agreed. "After all, *amore* means *love* in Italian."

So, Mama sat down on the floor next to Mia. Mama made hearts while Mia made art.

Mia drew a basketball for Grace because she loved to play.

She drew a rocket ship for Helen because she loved science.

Massimo loved trucks, so Mia drew one.

Olivia wanted a kitten, so Mia drew one with whiskers and eyes.

Bob slept with his baseball glove, so Mia drew a ball to go with it.

And Elsa, who spent every spare moment climbing the holly tree, got a squirrel. Mama hung the valentines inside the frames.

"They're funny." Mia Valentina giggled.

Mama checked the clock. "Oh no, we have to bake before everyone gets home!" she cried.

"Don't worry, Mama! I'll help!" Mia followed her mother into the kitchen.

Mia helped her mother measure the flour and sugar to sift into a mixing bowl. They mashed butter, cracked eggs, and poured milk into the bowl. Mama whipped the mixture. Mia helped pour the batter into the cupcake tin. Soon, the entire house smelled like vanilla.

It was time to make the frosting! Mama whisked the soft butter, sugar, and cream. Together they frosted and frosted and frosted until every cupcake had a smooth white cap. They sprinkled and sprinkled and sprinkled the frosting with pink sugar until every cupcake glittered.

Whomp! The kitchen door flew open!

One by one, Mia's brothers and sisters, Grace, Helen, Massimo, Olivia, Bob, and Elsa, poured into the house, followed by Papa, who was so tall and big, he brought the chill of the winter wind inside. Phyllis began to bark and run around the children as they peeled off their mittens and hung up their hats, scarves, and coats and Bob's baseball glove.

“How did it go?” Mama asked.

“We won!” Grace, the eldest and the tallest basketball player on her team, said proudly.

“Happy Valentine’s Day!” Papa exclaimed. “For you.” Papa gave Mama a gold box of chocolate-covered cherries along with a kiss.

"Time to decorate the kitchen door!" Mama opened the junk drawer. Helen grabbed one wheel of Scotch tape, Bob another, and Olivia another. Massimo gathered the loose paper valentines Mama had saved in the bottom of the bin. "Careful," Mama said in a loud voice. "These old valentines are family heirlooms."

The Amore children formed a shaky pyramid with Mia crawling to the top. The kitchen door was soon covered with the old valentines.

"Hey, kids, be careful," Papa chided them. "We aren't a circus act."

"Since when?" Mama winked.

As the pyramid collapsed, the pile of Amore children laughed.

"Mia, show the kids what you made in the parlor," Mama suggested.

The children ran to the parlor at once, causing a traffic jam. "Look! Roses everywhere!" Elsa twirled.

"And valentines." Mia pointed. The children laughed at their funny valentines, but no one noticed one was missing. No one had made Mia Valentina a valentine. She pretended not to be sad, but she was. The day with Mama had been so special, but could Mama really have forgotten about her?

"Time to set the table," Papa hollered. The children made a stampede and ran back to the kitchen.

Mama sat in the kitchen with her feet up and sampled a chocolate-covered cherry as Papa made the tomato sauce for the macaroni. Soon the polka-dot windows were fogged with steam as the pasta boiled on the stove.

The children set the table. Papa placed the macaroni, salad, and bread on the table. Mama lit the candles. The family sat down to

dinner as the gumdrop tree twinkled in the window and the stack of cupcakes shimmered on the counter.

Even though February 14th was Mia's favorite day, the valentine party just wasn't the same. Phyllis nudged Mia from her place under the table, as if she understood. After dinner and games, the seven Amore children took turns and stood at the bathroom mirror in their pajamas and scrubbed, brushed, and rinsed until they glistened. They hung their washcloths to dry on the antique tub with lion's feet.

Mia Valentina climbed into bed. She sunk into the soft mattress like a spoon in vanilla cake batter when she heard a crinkle. She sat up and lifted the blanket. But there was nothing under it. She lifted the sheet. There was nothing there either. She lifted her pillow. There it was! A valentine just for her!

Mia had not been forgotten after all. Tomorrow she'd ask Mama to make a frame and she would hang it in the parlor of roses with the others.

Phyllis jumped up onto Mia's bed. Mia grabbed the last two gumdrops and gave Phyllis the lavender one. She saved the red one for another day. Mia fell asleep with a smile on her face and her very own valentine in her hand.

The house on the hill didn't have the best heat or the newest wallpaper or windows with smooth glass, but it did have a candy tree, seven children full of macaroni and cupcakes, and enough valentines to wallpaper the world.

It only took one special holiday to make a house with stairs that creaked, doors that slammed, windows that whistled, and a parlor of roses become the House of Love. And, it turned out, there was so much love inside that there weren't enough rooms in the old house to hold it.

To My Valentine
STOP
In the Name of Love
"you BUTTER be mine"
BE MINE
I PICKED YOU
We make a PEACH of a Pear
You're Pur-r-r-fect!